Union

Union

Sara Cassidy

ORCA BOOK PUBLISHERS

Published in Canada and the United States
in 2022 by Orca Book Publishers.
orcabook.com

Library and Archives Canada Cataloguing in Publication
Title: Union / Sara Cassidy.
Names: Cassidy, Sara, author.
Identifiers: Canadiana (print) 20210382333 | Canadiana (ebook) 20210382341 |
ISBN 9781459834477 (softcover) | ISBN 9781459834484 (PDF) |
ISBN 9781459834491 (EPUB)
Classification: LCC PS8555.A7812 U55 2022 | DDC jc813/.54—dc23

Library of Congress Control Number: 2021950060

Summary: In this novel in verse for teen readers, fifteen-year-old Tuck navigates
new love, past trauma and standing up for what's right.

Orca Book Publishers is committed to reducing the consumption of
nonrenewable resources in the production of our books. We make
every effort to use materials that support a sustainable future.

Orca Book Publishers gratefully acknowledges the support
for its publishing programs provided by the following agencies:
the Government of Canada, the Canada Council for the Arts
and the Province of British Columbia through the BC Arts
Council and the Book Publishing Tax Credit.

Edited by Tanya Trafford
Cover artwork by Radha Joshi Raulgaonkar
Cover design by Rachel Page
Layout by Sydney Barnes

Printed and bound in Canada.

25 24 23 22 • 1 2 3 4

For survivors

Note: This novel alludes to sexual assault of a boy by a man (a mother's boyfriend). Readers may want to emotionally prepare.

Nape

Grace has caught my eye
I stare and stare
at this girl I've missed
since we were five

grade one
    grade two
        grade three
            grade four—

a girl
with a pink lunch box
black hair wound
in two braids

that's all I knew

then
she turned twelve
wove that hair
in one thick braid

that's it
that's all I saw
in the halls
up through the years
up the hill
to the big school
high school
where we are now

new hive
new crowd

grade nine

one week in
I'm lost

and found
with her
in the desk
in front of mine

dark hair
cut short
braid gone
neck bare

I fill
my lungs
take in air

breathe
all the way in
all the way out

for the first time

since

he—

Who

I fear
one day
I will be
the one in front
and she will see

that I am
not here

I am
hard bits
bone
plus bone
plus bone
plus bone
my spine
rung
on
rung

I am no more
than a bot

Hell

if she knew
what I have seen
what I have known
what I have done

how I can't dream—

she won't make room for me

I am filled
with scum
spume
sleaze
swill

I have choked
on hell

Job

This is what I need:
a job with hours
my name on a badge
a hat that says
I work here

shoes that do not slip
on grease
a smile on my face
bought by a wage

and when I get paid
I'll buy her fries
a game of pool
a live show

a job with hours
will take me
out of the house

far from its dust

its ghosts

Mom's slumps

my shame

Look

To Grace
I am still a boy
with a blue lunch box
blue jeans
a blue tee

a boy
on the thin side
white skin
two eyes
a nose
a mouth—

what's to tell?

all I ask
is that she looks at me
as long as it takes
for her

to see me

see her

Like

I scroll and flick
and like a dick
I like her post
with a click

oh yeah
I click

and the shape
of the heart
on the cold screen
fills
with bits
and bytes

and so it starts:
a "like"

a knock
a key

a beat

FAST FRANKS

I fill in a form
get hired on the spot
three shifts a week
Sat Sun Mon
2–6
each hour a box
where I can't get lost

I bathe, I wash, I shave
I ride the bus
I show up

Hi! I'm Tuck.
How can I help you?
Do you want fries with that?
Do you want to make it a large?
Do you want to buy two and get one free?

Do you want?
You want!
Let me get you what you want.

They tap their cards
pay their bills

the bags I hand them
are too light
for all that cash
the weight
of stale air
thin meat
warm Coke

they don't want
a real meal
they're here
to get off the couch
give their heads a shake
a change of pace
to get a smile
a *have a nice day*
a bag with its top rolled down

all they have to do is pay
that's the deal
it comes cheap—

the boss
won't let us take
tips
they go in a box
for dogs
who are lost

Fez

I tell Fez
how rude they are
how they think they get
what they want
but have learned to take
what they don't need

You think too much, Fez says
since your dad left

Not my dad, I snarl

Right
your mom's fling
that stayed
do you miss him?

the world goes dark
my throat stings
a dark ball
fills the space
where my ribs meet
I try to breathe
sip air

Hey, I say
Do you know Grace?

Yeah, Fez says
the one with braids?

It's short now
an edge bob
with a shaved side
the right side

Fez laughs
Sounds like you've had a good long look

I sing it to him then
how she's fun and smart
and sure but shy
how she runs deep
moves sleek
I say her name
ten times at least
shape it new
set it free

a bird in flight
seed in bloom
star in the sky
shimmering

You've got it bad, says Fez

Sum

Math class
Grace looks up
from her phone
and it's
the best sum:
eye to eye
one to one
Tuck plus Grace
Grace plus Tuck

time goes weak
slows right down

Grace nods quick
puts her thumb
to her lip
stares at her phone
but does not scroll

now I'm the one
to be met
for the first time

the one

who saw her first

in this new life

Check

The first check is not
what I thought it would be
the law lets them pay
half the wage
while we learn the job
it's strange math
as if we're half
at work

then there's the tax
they take
which, I know, pays
for roads and schools
good things
but when there's zip
to start with
it's a large clip

Jeff the fry cook
claps me on the back
stare and stare, he says
but it won't grow
I have three jobs

to pay my rent
some days
I'm on the bus
more hours
than I work
job to job to job
to pay rent on a pad
where all I do
is sleep it off
or stare at the air
see
if they give you more
than five hours in a row
they'd have to pay you
to stop for a meal
they'd have to pay you
when you get sick
go on a trip
get your teeth cleaned
so
they duck the law
with short shifts
short shrift
paid time off?
that would be a dream

but my dream
is their loss
their cost
but hey Tuck
you're young
have fun
spend the dough
on dumb stuff
just don't get stuck
in a place like this—
stay in school

Jeff lifts a rack of fries
from hot oil
his wrists stained
as if by rain
a braille
of grease burns

you hear me?
stay in school
if you need help, ask
there's no shame
it's not my fault
that my brain

flipped ink
on its head
they called me slow
they did not see
how my gears whirl!
I go on and on hey?
hours on a bus
give you time to think

Game Time

In class
Grace tells Liz
loud and clear
I'll be at the game at noon
then looks
my way

Fez texts then:
can you keep score?
we're short

I text back: *noon game?*

Fez texts: 👍

so I was meant
to be there
when Grace walks in
with Liz and Jen

I'm scared I'll miss
a point
mess up the board

but more I fear
that through the noise
of the game and crowd
she'll hear
the real game ball
my heart
as it knocks and knocks

I dare
to look at her
at all of her

she has
her eyes on me
on all of me

just us
in that big room

Trix

So I'm at the frame—
that's what we call
the square in the wall
we hand meals through
to the folks in their cars
who roll on past
like queens and czars

this woman
with quick eyes
drives up
for one thing:
black tea

no one goes to FAST FRANKS
for one thing

it's an old car
with two phones on the dash
books in the back
she's Mom's age
but makes Mom look
like she took a wrong road

to a dead end
thick with dust

Are you Tuck?
she asks
her voice low
I'm Trix

does she want to sell me drugs
or what?

Jeff gave me your name
you've heard of the FAST FRANKS
in Port Lang?

I shake my head

Last month
the staff there
joined our
union
now they meet with the boss
to work out new rules
to have their needs met
to get some rights

Rights? I ask

Yeah
like they can't get fired if they miss a shift
and can choose to wear
the pants or the skirt—
it's their choice
they can be gay, trans
can get full shifts
paid breaks
sick days
child care on site
eye tests
teeth filled
good pay
safe work
a job they can
live on
and
live with

she takes her tea
do you know what a union is?

I do, I say

The jerk would grunt
fat cats
if they were on the news
so I looked them up
unions are why
kids go to school
and don't go blind at looms
or break their backs down mines
unions are why
we get two days off each week

They're so
you don't give up your life, I say
to get by day to day

Trix beams
Jeff said you were smart
and that you're liked here
my hope is you'll talk
with the folks you work with
see where they stand
make a list of who
would join the fight
and who

would run and tell the boss
talk to those on the fence
let them know
they can have a voice
and change their lives

Why not Jeff? I ask

Trix shakes her head
Jeff has too much on the line
he'd have no home if he lost this job
you're young
you live at home, right?
we'd train you
you could change lives

I'm in, I say
a thrill runs through me

but then
I feel like a fool
mocked
who do I think I am?

great, Trix says

when she drives off
I'm full bot
I ring up bills
make change
thank you
have a nice night

a   nice   night

I pour hot tea
on my wrist

to feel

relief

that will leave
a scar

Work

I cut, chop, slice.
The knife they give me is sharp.
I lift bags.
I sink fries
in hot oil.
Cut, chop, slice.
Four hours straight.
No break.
Cut, chop, slice.
It's all I'm asked to do.
It's all I need to do.
No one asks for more.
Cut, chop, slice.
Four hours filled.
And when I need to think
I think of Grace.

Check Two

I take check two
to the bank

a full wage
now that I'm trained

put it in the slot
it's still not a lot

the bot spits it out
in cash:

six bills
slick as silk

I fold them so they're thick

I'll buy Grace a rose—
a stick
and poke

Fez has ink

♥
—

She hearts my post!
A shot of the sun
as it fell to the sea
like a drop of hot oil

I snapped the pic
on my way home
from the stick and poke
a new rose stung
on my wrist
as if stitched
in place by
its own thorns

her "like"
soothes the sting
through the gauze
through the screen

a salve, a balm

calm

Squad

Trix picks me up
at the end of my shift
we park at Ross Bay
and watch the waves
rain beads the air
and ticks on the car roof

Trix has brought hot tea
and Mars bars
paid for by the union

All you have to do
is talk it up
get folks on board
who you can trust
ask them
to spread the word
you know how it is:
I told two friends
and they told two friends...
it adds up fast
once half the staff
want the right

to what they need
we'll have them sign
union cards
one at a time
then all the staff
—not just the ones on board—
will vote
to join or not
to be a group
a team, a squad
a big step up
from droid

How It Starts

This is how it goes
this is how it grows

we get to class:
nod
nod

we pass in the hall:
hi
hi

at the school doors at three:
hey
hey

on the screen:
Like
Like
Like
Like
Like
"nice"
"ha"

I slide in
Did you get your mark back on the math quiz?
smooth!
I wait

I add:
I messed up that part where $E = MC^2$
I thought it was cubed
damn that was nuts but too late now
I wait

I wait

I wait and wait and wait and wait

make sure my phone is on
the sound up

go for a run
take a bath
bite my nails
wish I could
take it back
think I might change schools—

bzzzz

a chime
gold coin, flash of light

I eye my phone
I take it slow
my sweat brims cold
here we go

LOL i did fine on that part it was the 2+2 that sank me

I don't have to think
I just type:
*yeah that one was tough
and not in our notes*

*i know—
she sprang it on us*

a pause

Me: *hehe*

pause

Grace: *I got an A.*
Me: *You did?!*
Grace: 👉 💡
Me: *Me too.* 😊
Grace: 🧹
Me: 🎉

× ÷ + −

=

∞

Grace: ∞

Break Room

I talk low
I nudge, hint, prod
I get to know
the front staff
the cooks
the night guards
What do you think of the pay? I ask
Do you like the hours?
Do you feel safe?
What would make work good for you?
What would make it worth it?

they don't know what I'm up to
but once I can trust them
I turn the light on

I did not know I could be sly like this
I text Grace one night

come on, she texts back
you're sly as a fox

did you say I'm a fox?

ha ha i guess i did

one day Jeff walks in
as I talk it up
with Minh, a prep cook
who's had the same pay
for three years
not one raise
and four kids to feed
when Minh's off work
he drives cab
mows lawns

Jeff gives me a thumbs-up
backs out of the room
Minh does not look like Jeff
but he is like him:
three jobs
scars on his hands

then the boss walks in
looks right through me
just the new kid
nods at Minh
says:
How are ya, Mike?

A Date

Grace and I text each night
but in school it's still
hey
hey

at night I learn
she has dance class
three times a week
her dad works up north on an oil rig
she has met him three times
four if you count the day i was born

it's just her and her mom
same as it's just me and mine
is your mom on her own? I ask *does she date?*

she tried but no luck
yours?

my throat goes dry
she had a bad dude for a while
but he's gone now
I type

the room spins
the first time
comes to mind
his hand on me
as I reached
for a cup—
a grab
as if I was
dough, clay
three years on
I still freeze
seize
stop
watch
wait
doubt

oh Grace says

do you want to get lunch? I blurt

I planned to ask YOU that

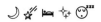

∞

∞

Kiss

we kiss
!!!
lip to lip
tongue to tongue
one small clack of teeth

we share lunch
at the Thai place
talk the whole time
the way we text—
with flow

speak hear ask laugh say tease push let

we walk back to school
on the old path through the park
with the tire swing
she hops on
then I jump on
and we spin
as if from
a bolt of silk
she reaches up

I lean in
and we kiss
spin
kiss
spin

then I froze
my mouth went dry
I pulled back

we have to get to class

yeah
that's what I said
I am a jerk
I'm not worth
her
not worth
the taste of joy

at ten
the screen is blank

but then

hey she texts

click click click
our phones in the dark
that same flow
we've come to know
the night's best show

so we kissed
and I messed it up
but we kissed

Rights

Would you like
the right
to
good pay?
full hours?

they nod
"of course"
they fist bump
or high five
like they've dreamed
of this

but some
shake their heads
one says
I'm old
all I know
is we're stuck
with this shit

we aren't stuck, I say
we can change it

The guy laughs
then looks
through my eyes
as if to check
that I have a soul

Don't shit me, he says

Why would I do that? I ask
I spread out my palms
to show I have no tricks
I stand tall
to show I know what to do
that I'll lead the way
that we'll all be fine

though of course
I do not know what to do
I can't lead
my own self out
from my own hell
I will not be fine

Where do I sign, the guy asks

It should be soon, I say
but could you talk to Saul and Dar?
see if they're in?
they'll need a push
you will have to be sly

Oh I will be sly
the guy winks
he points to the badge on his sleeve
ha! the dude's name is Sly

we laugh and laugh

like fam

More

Who dropped you off? Mom asks

I tell Mom who Trix is
our fight for rights
for folks
who work long hours
for loose change
while the boss counts bills

Don't do this, Mom says
You'll lose your job.
You'll have a mark by your name.
Keep your head down.
Bite your tongue.
Son this is how the world works.
Some get rich, most stay poor.
You've got food, a roof.
Don't ask for more.

Mom I need more
than food and a roof
I need to feel
that my work is seen

the time I have is scarce
like gold is scarce
like silk is scarce

Mom no one is worth more
no one is worth less

I stop—
well, one guy is

Who? Mom asks

Phil, I say
I push past her
charge to my room

It Comes Back

It all comes back
I thought it was in the past

now that I know Grace
and walk on air

thought I was free
in the clear

it all comes back
the bad comes back

his hand on me
when he got the chance

his long reach
nights I tried to sleep

and the creep
would knock and knock

say he just had to talk
that he'd give me cash

and that if I told, he'd say
I was the one who "asked for it"

how I'd freeze and wait
how I still can't breathe

so when Grace says
she loves me

I choke

Skate Park

You got the girl!
Fez says

                                                    Yeah
                                          but I messed it up
                                    she said those three words
                                                    and—
—*you did not say them back*

                                                    yup

aw, man
she must be mad

                                          Fez, can't you—

—*be your friend and lie?*
say that she won't care?
that it's fine to lose her?
there's lots of fish in the sea?

                              I don't tell him
                              that last night

Grace did not text
that I sent three
then knew to leave it

all you have to do
is say the three words back

I can't

why not?

because then
she'd be stuck with me

and you'll be stuck with her
and the stars will shine
and you'll hold hands and glow
and all the kids will know

Tuck that's how it works!

I shrug
Fez smiles

but I can't

I can't make her a part of this

can't let the tar and grime
the mire and lye
of what I know
stick to her

Boss

The boss glares
cuts my hours
gives me day shifts
so I miss school
hands me the mop
puts me on dish pit
docks my pay
when I don't wear my hat

But he won't fire you, Jeff says
he knows you have friends
and that we'd
put a wrench in his works
we'd botch the cheese sauce
steal from the till
work slow
he can't risk that—
we could bring this place down
he sees now
he needs us
just like
we need him

good work, kid

Stuck

She will think that
she did me wrong
that it's her fault
I did not sing back

or worse—
she will feel
she is not kind
or smart or fun

I'm stuck

I have to tell her
what I did
that I went weak
that I tried to shrink
that I begged the air
that I prayed to a wall
that I did not scream
that I would have died

I still can't breathe
I still can't move

and if I speak
she'd know the truth
that I'm not
what she sees
that I'm a fake
that I'm not right

if she loves me
she has to know me
but if she knows me
how can she love me

Net

Large fries,
ranch on the side.

my heart stops
my ribs knot

that was his thing—
fries and ranch dip

I look through the frame
but it's not him
of course it's not
he's gone
long gone
I know that

I guess fear
casts a wide net
so I'm still prey
that's fear's way
to keep me safe
it ramps me up
and pins me down

don't move, it says
don't say a word

The Things He Took

It's one year to the day
I got home from school
and he was gone
no note for Mom
not one word
took the car

What can I do? Mom said
It's his car.
He pays each month.

he took her set of keys too
took some cans of beans
took a sleeping bag
took a bar of soap
a bike lock
a charge cord—

the signs that he was gone
were the things he took

*

that same day he left
I'd planned to tell her
why I would not greet him
or make small talk at meals
why I was *such a shit*
as he'd put it

I had planned
to say these words:

He comes to my room at night.

That was all I would need to say
it would be
clear as day
what he asked for
in the dark

did he know my plan?
did he know me so well?

but I did not say a word
as Mom went room to room
in search of a warm clue
to prove—

what?
that he would miss her?

she sank to the floor
saw the stark truth
I was no one to him.

and I bit my tongue
so that it bled
but it did not hurt

It's Time

It's time, Trix says
*we'll rent a space
give folks a day
to stop in and sign
their union cards*

We're in her car
on the point
the tea is hot and sweet
my list of names is in her hands
green check marks
the odd red X

You've done great work, Trix says
you should be proud

my heart bobs
then
it
sinks
a star
burned out

thanks, I say
a grunt

Her eyes track
my thumb
on my wrist
as I trace
the stem of my rose
the tips of its thorns

you good?

                              I'm good

you sure?
it makes sense to be scared
but you've got lots of names here
they'll sign the cards
then in two weeks we'll do a vote
this will go through
I know it

                              yeah

I stare at the sea
the pulse of the waves
the foam on their peaks
I dig my nails in
score my skin

Trix shifts in her seat
looks at me

and school? all good?

I nod

and home?

it's small

a flinch:

my head shifts
to the right
to the left

Heard

Trix puts down her tea
she turns off her phone
puts it on the dash, screen down
her eyes are still for the first time
she lines them up with mine

We don't have to do the cards now, she says
we can put it off
we can put it all off
if you need time
to deal with stuff

I bite my lip
I taste blood

Do you want to talk?

My head shifts
to the right
to the left

Not yet, Trix says, *I get that*
but Tuck I have to ask

are you safe?

my head goes up
my head goes down

Good, Trix says
I won't make you talk
if you can't
but I know it would help

I cry then
a warm cry
that leaves me stung
clean as if I've been
scrubbed with salt

I have a friend, Trix says
that I see once a week

a shrink? I ask

sort of, Trix says
a counsellor
she can't solve your pain
but she can help

so you don't push it down
she'll show you
how to take charge of it
how to live with it
I'll text you her deets
and guess what?
the union might pay

Test

hey
hey

I have to tell you this thing

kk

it will test us

kk

what we have
could shift
to low gear

kk
you know i'm good at tests :)

∞

∞

The Place

I choose a place I do not know
a small park far from home
trees I can stain
leaves I can stun

we sit like old folks
take the whole bench
I can't be near her
can't let her catch
what I am spoiled with
I place my hands
on my knees
bow my head
as if I'll spew

tell me
she says
I'm scared
she says

I thought I would
spill it out
cry and wail—

but I go full bot
I stutter
start and stop

it's the hardest work I've ever done
harder than a marathon
harder than a 10-hour shift
to say twelve words

my mother's boyfriend...

I sit in shock
burn in shame
the words I've said
a cloud of gnats
at my ears
freed from my brain

Grace waits
can you tell me more

I try
but I shake my head

Grace looks at the sky

takes a deep breath

I hate him, she says
she makes a fist
where does he live?

that makes me laugh
it feels so good
in my throat
to laugh

she holds me
I melt
she holds me and holds me
I weep

Mom

Grace texts that night
asks the thing I can't face:
does your mom know?

I want to run
I try to breathe
I stare at the hole
I once clawed in the wall

Grace waits
I'm safe
my phone clicks
in the dark
as I write
strokes of light:
she's too hurt
i can't hurt her more

Grace texts back:
she needs to know

i don't think so, I type
why add to her grief?

not yet then, Grace texts

not now, I text back

∞

∞

Cards

The bar down the block
is part of the union
and gives us the keys for the day
Trix brings cans of pop
date squares
pens in cups
a stack of union cards

an hour ticks past
no one comes
the bar is dark and cool
it starts to feel grim
Trix eyes the gin
and jokes
I could use a shot

Hey!
It's dark in here
Jeff bursts in
Where do I sign?
Am I the first?

Not if I beat you to it—
Sly slips in

then there's a line of them
Can I keep the pen?
My mom would be proud.
This is the good fight.

the cards fill up
Trix gets more from her car
I did not want to hope, she says

You aimed low? I ask

I aimed for half of you to sign
but it looks like all of you will!

and then we're done

Thanks, Tuck!
Right on, man.
You rock.
Give me five.
You're the bomb!
We owe you.
It's the U and I in union that makes us strong!

Counsellor

She tells me
I'm not the first kid
that has been through this
that they froze too
it was all we could do
to make it through

she says
I have more strength
than I know

I say
it's my fault

she asks
does it help you
to think that way?

the ball presses
against my ribs
makes me
want to vomit

stops me
from breathing

it keeps me where he put me, I say

she teaches me
how to calm

I name things
I see, hear, smell, feel

she tells me
I can visualize

I take the heavy ball in my hands
crush it into dust
she opens the window
and as I throw it out
a breeze gusts up
and carries it away

my ribs loosen
I inhale
exhale
inhale
exhale

long, slow breaths
like stitches through cloth
returning me
to earth

It will come and go, the counsellor says
this feeling, this healing
it will start to stay whole days
then whole months
then entire years—
you will be well
you will be yourself

we plan to meet
once a week
in that warm room
where I am safe
where I can speak

I run home
light
with all of me
the whole of me

Three Words

By the time
I say
the three words
they're obvious

as I prepare
to say them
Grace smiles
leans in
to kiss me
I love you I say quickly
before our lips touch

love you too she mumbles

three beads of sound
that thread the world
through our hearts
back to itself

a river
runs through me now

holding me together
ligament and vein

and if some of it is poison
it is my own blood
that I pump clean
with every beat

my stomach growls
Grace laughs
let's get something to eat she says

Yeah I say
but not just yet

I'm happy

happy to be hungry
to have my own hunger
and to be with Grace
in this buoyant moment
of forgiven time

Acknowledgments

I am grateful to Tanya Trafford and sensitivity reader Melanie Siebert for their deep attention to this text.

Sara Cassidy is a writer and editor. Her children's books have been shortlisted for many awards, including the Governor General's Literary Award, the Bolen Books Children's Book Prize, the Silver Birch Express Award, the Ruth and Sylvia Schwartz Children's Book Award, the Rocky Mountain Book Award and the Chocolate Lily Award. Most recently, she won the Sheila A. Egoff Children's Literature Prize for her chapter book *Genius Jolene*. Sara also writes nonfiction and poetry for adults. She lives in Victoria, British Columbia.

SEVENTEEN-YEAR-OLD GRETA doesn't have high expectations for her last year of high school. When she blacks out at a party she thinks that it can't get any worse. She's wrong.

While Greta deals with the confusion and shame of that night, her stepmother and father choose that moment to disappear, abandoning Greta and her twin brother, Ash. Alone and broke, Greta and Ash need to find a way to make it through the harsh Edmonton winter.

"Subtle and nuanced...takes readers on an unapologetic journey of family, trauma and the transformative power of kindness."

—NATASHA DEEN, author of *In the Key of Nira Ghani*

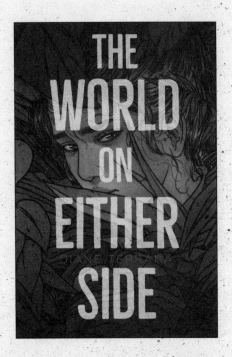

AFTER THE DEATH OF HER BOYFRIEND, sixteen-year-old Valentine shuts down completely. Desperate for her daughter to recover, Valentine's mother takes her on a trek in Thailand. In the mountains north of Chiang Mai, Valentine meets Lin, a young elephant keeper with a hidden past, and an orphaned elephant calf, pursued by violent poachers. Together, the three flee into the jungle, looking for refuge and redemption.

"A work of refreshing moral complexity about characters seeking atonement and redemption—and finding the courage it takes to love and to live."

—TRILBY KENT, Governor General's Literary Award finalist for *Once, in a Town Called Moth*

HOW FAR WE GO AND HOW FAST

NORA DECTER

JOLENE COMES FROM A LONG LINE of musical lowlifes. It's Jolene and her big brother, Matt, who are the true musicians. When they write songs together, everything seems better. But when Matt up and leaves in the middle of the night, Jo loses her only friend and support system. As it becomes clear that Matt is never coming back, Jo turns to music to navigate her loss.